I'M A LEEDS UNITED SUPERFAN!

THE OFFICIAL
LEEDS
UNITED
ANNUAL 2014

Written by John Wray

Photography:
Andrew Varley Picture Agency

Great Northern Books
PO Box 213, Ilkley, LS29 9WS
www.greatnorthernbooks.co.uk

© Leeds United FC

Design and layout: David Burrill

ISBN: 978-0-9576399-1-1

CIP Data
A catalogue for this book is available
from the British Library

GREAT NORTHERN

£8

Contents

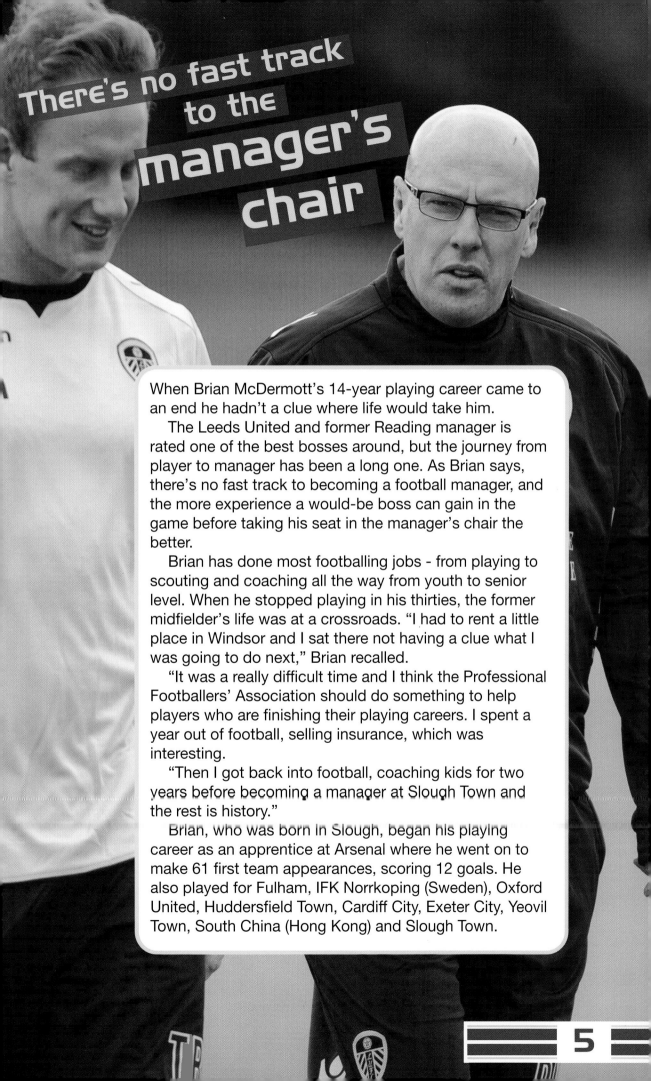

There's no fast track to the manager's chair

When Brian McDermott's 14-year playing career came to an end he hadn't a clue where life would take him.

The Leeds United and former Reading manager is rated one of the best bosses around, but the journey from player to manager has been a long one. As Brian says, there's no fast track to becoming a football manager, and the more experience a would-be boss can gain in the game before taking his seat in the manager's chair the better.

Brian has done most footballing jobs - from playing to scouting and coaching all the way from youth to senior level. When he stopped playing in his thirties, the former midfielder's life was at a crossroads. "I had to rent a little place in Windsor and I sat there not having a clue what I was going to do next," Brian recalled.

"It was a really difficult time and I think the Professional Footballers' Association should do something to help players who are finishing their playing careers. I spent a year out of football, selling insurance, which was interesting.

"Then I got back into football, coaching kids for two years before becoming a manager at Slough Town and the rest is history."

Brian, who was born in Slough, began his playing career as an apprentice at Arsenal where he went on to make 61 first team appearances, scoring 12 goals. He also played for Fulham, IFK Norrkoping (Sweden), Oxford United, Huddersfield Town, Cardiff City, Exeter City, Yeovil Town, South China (Hong Kong) and Slough Town.

His first step on the managerial ladder was made at Slough where he became player-manager in 1995. Success wasn't immediate and when Slough hit serious cash problems, Brian lost his job, along with most of the players. After a spell in charge at Woking and losing his job there too, he joined Reading as chief scout in September, 2000. He also took charge of the club's Under 19 and reserve teams before becoming manager in 2009.

After Reading lost out on promotion in the play-off final against Swansea City in 2011, they went on to climb into the Premiership a year later and Brian was named Championship Manager of the Year by the League Managers' Association.

They say the only certainty in a manager's career (unless he happens to be Sir Alex Ferguson!) is the sack - and Reading parted company with Brian in March, 2013, after four successive league defeats.

Reading's loss was Leeds United's gain as Brian was appointed at Elland Road in April, 2013, with a three-year contract. He said: "My advice to any player who wants to be a manager is to take the coaching badges, do a bit of scouting and stay in a footballing environment. Because I've done most jobs at a football club I can relate to the people around the training ground.

"It doesn't necessarily mean you are going to be a great football manager just because you've been a top player. Jose Mourinho, for instance, had a modest playing career, but look at his achievements in coaching and management. Anyone keen to stay in football beyond his playing career has to stay positive because something will come along."

So what makes a good manager? Brian grins: "A bloke who wins games. That's the only thing that matters. You can be the best man-manager in the world but if you don't win matches you won't stay in the job. You need luck too, determination to succeed and a lot of hard work."

Paddy
KENNY

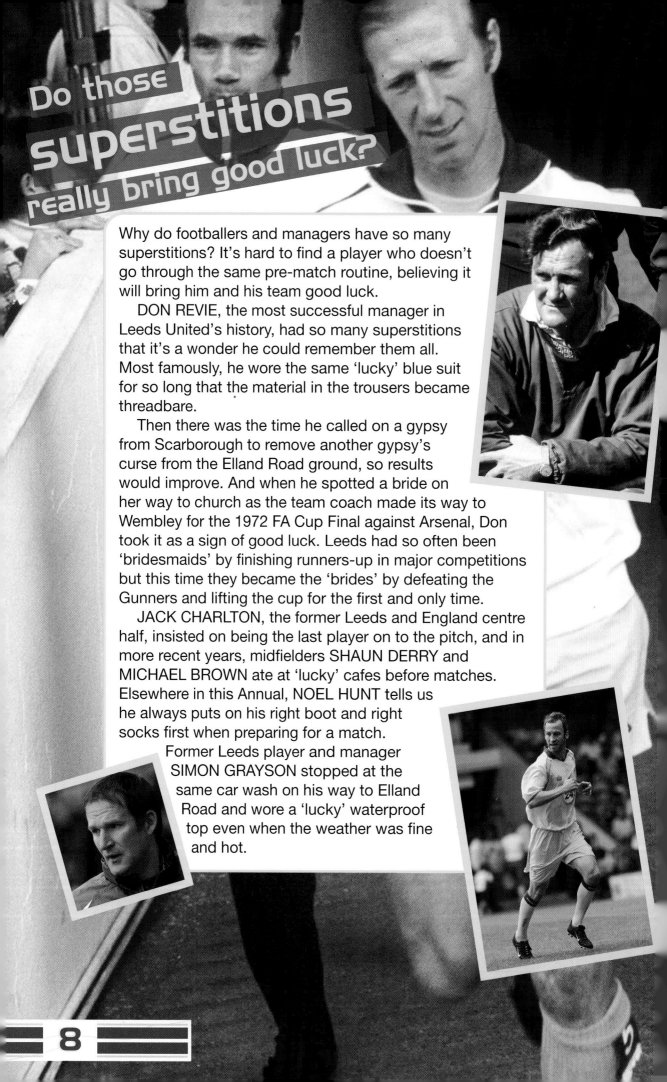

Do those superstitions really bring good luck?

Why do footballers and managers have so many superstitions? It's hard to find a player who doesn't go through the same pre-match routine, believing it will bring him and his team good luck.

DON REVIE, the most successful manager in Leeds United's history, had so many superstitions that it's a wonder he could remember them all. Most famously, he wore the same 'lucky' blue suit for so long that the material in the trousers became threadbare.

Then there was the time he called on a gypsy from Scarborough to remove another gypsy's curse from the Elland Road ground, so results would improve. And when he spotted a bride on her way to church as the team coach made its way to Wembley for the 1972 FA Cup Final against Arsenal, Don took it as a sign of good luck. Leeds had so often been 'bridesmaids' by finishing runners-up in major competitions but this time they became the 'brides' by defeating the Gunners and lifting the cup for the first and only time.

JACK CHARLTON, the former Leeds and England centre half, insisted on being the last player on to the pitch, and in more recent years, midfielders SHAUN DERRY and MICHAEL BROWN ate at 'lucky' cafes before matches. Elsewhere in this Annual, NOEL HUNT tells us he always puts on his right boot and right socks first when preparing for a match.

Former Leeds player and manager SIMON GRAYSON stopped at the same car wash on his way to Elland Road and wore a 'lucky' waterproof top even when the weather was fine and hot.

NEIL WARNOCK, Grayson's successor as manager, had one of the most unusual superstitions of all, stopping at every traffic light on his way home, whether it was showing red or green! One of Warnock's other quirks was refusing to watch when a penalty was being taken by one of his players.

Superstitions have been just as common at other clubs down the years. West Ham defender BOBBY MOORE, who captained England to the World Cup in 1966, would wait until all his team-mates had put their shorts on before putting on his own.

TV presenter and former England and Leicester striker GARY LINEKER would never practise shooting during the pre-match warm-up because he didn't want to waste his best shots at goal. Argentine legend DIEGO MARADONA held rosary beads in his hands during games and whenever his team switched training pitches he made the sign of the cross.

Blackpool manager and former England international PAUL INCE would wait until he was on the pitch before putting his shirt on, and Spanish international keeper PEPE REINA, loaned out by Liverpool to Napoli, fills up with petrol before every match, whether he needs it or not!

Tottenham and England's JERMAINE DEFOE has a close-cropped haircut before every game because he always seemed to get injured when he wore his hair longer. JOHN TERRY, Chelsea's former England captain, occupies the same seat on the team coach and former England keeper DAVID JAMES won't talk to anyone before a match.

Finally, let's hope former England winger CHRIS WADDLE had a good laundry during his time at Newcastle United because he wore the same pair of underpants throughout the 1982-83 season – again for good luck!

So you want to be a captain

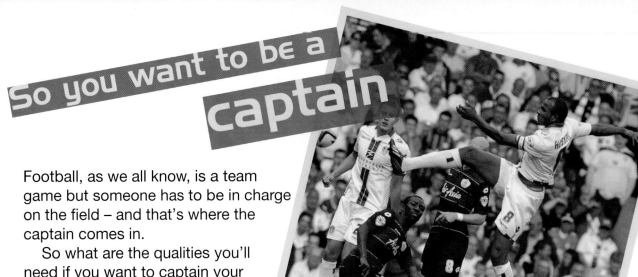

Football, as we all know, is a team game but someone has to be in charge on the field – and that's where the captain comes in.

So what are the qualities you'll need if you want to captain your team? Rodolph Austin was handed the armband at Leeds United for the 2013-14 season and he has some sound advice for anyone wanting to be a skipper.

"You have to show respect to your team-mates and set an example by training well, playing well and showing good discipline," he says. "You need to encourage people around you. You can't put them down or go around shouting at them – that's not me at all."

Rodolph refuses to put himself under too much pressure as captain, arguing: "It's just an armband. Football is a team game, not an individual one, so ideally you want 11 captains in a team, all helping each other out."

Although he had captained Jamaica's under 20s and occasionally skippered his country's senior team and his Norwegian club side SK Brann once or twice, Rodolph got a shock when manager Brian McDermott asked him to captain Leeds United. He explained: "I was surprised because Pelts (Lee Peltier) had done a good job as captain and Greenie (Paul Green) was captain in most of the pre-season games.

"I wasn't expecting it but I accepted it after some thought. Although captaining Leeds United is a huge honour, it is a big responsibility. So I asked the manager for a bit of time to consider because I am not the kind of person to jump into decisions."

Jamaicans love cricket, of course, and Rodolph captained his high school's cricket team. The strong-tackling midfielder grew up next to a football pitch and spent many hours playing there with his pals, but he always had a passion for cricket.

And he became so good with bat and ball that eventually he had to choose between a career in cricket or football.

"I played a lot of cricket and still love it," said Rodolph. "When I go home on holidays I try to visit the nets and do a bit of bowling and batting. I had to choose because I could have taken up either sport as a career, to be honest, but I did very well at football in my last year at high school and got called up for Jamaica's national under 20 team.

"When we went to Germany to play, I did very well there too and was picked for Jamaica's senior squad in 2004."

Rodolph loves to lead by example and he believes he can trace his strong tackling back to childhood when he was always up against bigger boys on that football pitch overlooking his home. He also built up his strength by swimming in the nearby river and spent most of the day playing sport before arriving home with a huge appetite.

Rodolph made an impressive start to his Leeds career, scoring some spectacular goals, and says his debut goal against Oxford at Elland Road in the Capital One Cup gave him most satisfaction. He admits his form dipped on his return from a cracked ankle bone, received in the 6-1 home defeat by Watford in November, 2012, but he worked hard to improve and celebrated his first game as captain, a goalless draw at Leicester in August, 2013, by winning the Man of the Match champagne.

Manager McDermott said: "It was typical of Rudy that he came into the dressing room with the bottle of champagne, said 'that's for all of us' and shook everybody's hand. That's the kind of guy he is – a real competitor and team man."

JOHN CHARLES

Most league goals in a season – 42 in 1953-4.

Date of birth: December 27, 1931.
Place of birth: Swansea.
Died: February 24, 2004 (aged 72).
Also played centre half.
Leeds career: 1948-57 and 1962.
Leeds appearances: 327.
Goals: 157.
Wales: 38 caps, 15 goals.
Other clubs: Swansea Town (youth), Juventus, Roma, Cardiff City, Hereford United, Merthyr Tydfil.

Super

MARK VIDUKA

Scored four goals against Liverpool in November, 2000.

Date of birth: October 9, 1975.
Place of birth: Melbourne.
Leeds career: 2000-2004.
Leeds appearances: 166.
Leeds goals: 72 goals.
Australia: 43 caps, 11 goals.
Other clubs: AIS (youth), Melbourne Croatia Knights, Croatia Zagreb, Celtic, Middlesbrough, Newcastle United.

JOE JORDAN

Fearsome striker for Leeds and Scotland.

Date of birth: December 15, 1951.
Place of birth: Carluke, Scotland.
Leeds career: 1970-78.
Leeds appearances: 220.
Leeds goals: 46.
Scotland: 52 caps, 11 goals.
Other clubs: Morton, Manchester United, Milan, Hellas Verona, Southampton, Bristol City.

LEE CHAPMAN

Goal at Bournemouth sealed promotion in 1990.

Date of birth: December 5, 1959.
Place of birth: Lincoln.
Leeds career: 1990-93 and 1996 (loan).
Leeds appearances: 174.
Leeds goals: 79.
Other clubs: Stoke City, Plymouth (on loan), Arsenal, Sunderland, Sheffield Wednesday, Niortais, Nottingham Forest, Portsmouth, West Ham, Southend (on loan), Ipswich Town, Swansea City, Stromgodset IF.

ALLAN CLARKE

Nickname 'Sniffer' for sniffing out goals. Scored against Arsenal to win the FA Cup in 1972.

Date of birth: July 31, 1946.
Place of birth: Willenhall.
Leeds career: 1969-78.
Leeds appearances: 364.
Leeds goals: 151.
England: 19 caps, 10 goals.
Other clubs: Walsall, Fulham, Leicester City, Barnsley.

Strikers

JIMMY FLOYD HASSELBAINK

Joint winner of the Golden Boot for scoring 18 Premiership goals for Leeds in 1000-9.

Date of birth: March 27, 1972.
Place of birth: Paramaribo, Surinam.
Leeds career: 1997-99.
Leeds appearances: 87.
Leeds goals: 42.
Holland: 23 caps, 9 goals.
Other clubs: Telstar, AZ, Campomaiorese, Boavista, Atletico Madrid, Chelsea, Middlesbrough, Charlton Athletic, Cardiff City.

Wizard of the dribble. In 1965 became the first black player to turn out in an FA Cup Final.

Date of birth: March 13, 1940.
Place of birth: Germiston, South Africa.
Died: September 28, 1995 (aged 55).
Leeds career: 1960-70.
Leeds appearances: 200.
Leeds goals: 67.
Other clubs: York City.

ALBERT JOHANNESEN

Midfield

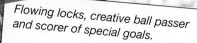

Flowing locks, creative ball passer and scorer of special goals.

Date of birth: January 1, 1950.
Place of birth: Edgware.
Leeds career: 1976-79.
Leeds appearances: 124.
Leeds goals: 16.
England: 17 caps, 3 goals.
Other clubs: Watford, Sheffield United, Queens Park Rangers, Southend United, Torquay United, Stockport County.

TONY CURRIE

and
Wingers

Bundle of energy who captained Leeds to the 1989-90 Second Division title and the 1991-92 First Division title.

Date of birth: February 9, 1957.
Place of birth: Edinburgh.
Leeds career: 1989-95.
Leeds appearances: 244.
Leeds goals: 43.
Scotland: 50 caps, 5 goals.
Other clubs: Dundee, Aberdeen, Manchester United, Coventry City.

GORDON STRACHAN

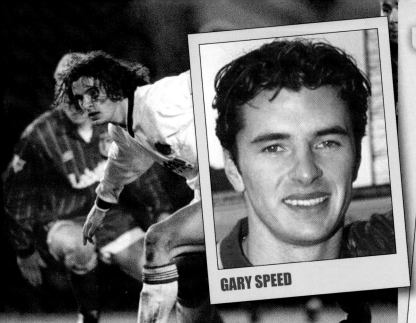

GARY SPEED

Superb header and striker of the ball. Member of Leeds' First Division title winning team in 1992.

Date of birth: September 8, 1969.
Place of birth: Mancot, Wales.
Died: November 27, 2011 (aged 42)
Leeds career: 1984-96.
Leeds appearances: 311
Leeds goals: 57.
Wales: 85 caps, 7 goals.
Other clubs: Everton, Newcastle United, Bolton Wanderers, Sheffield United.

Maestros

BILLY BREMNER

Greatest captain in Leeds United's history. Would run through a brick wall for the club. Scorer of vital goals in the glorious Don Revie era.

Date of birth: December 9, 1942.
Place of birth: Stirling.
Died: December 7, 1997 (aged 54).
Leeds career: 1959-76.
Leeds appearances: 772.
Leeds goals: 115.
Scotland: 54 caps, 3 goals.
Other clubs: Hull City, Doncaster Rovers.

JOHN SHERIDAN

Crowd favourite who always gave 100 per cent effort during the 1980s.

Date of birth: October 1, 1964.
Place of birth: Stretford.
Leeds career: 1982-89.
Leeds appearances: 264.
Leeds goals: 52.
Republic of Ireland: 34 caps, 5 goals.
Other clubs: Manchester City, Nottingham Forest, Sheffield Wednesday, Birmingham City (loan), Bolton Wanderers (loan), Doncaster Rovers, Oldham Athletic.

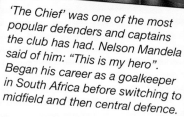

FRANK GRAY

Younger brother of Eddie Gray, the dependable left back played in Leeds' European Cup Final defeat to Bayern Munich in 1975 but won the European Cup with Nottingham Forest in 1980.

Date of birth: October 27, 1954.
Place of birth: Glasgow.
Position: Left back.
Leeds career: 1972-79, 1981-85.
Leeds appearances: 405.
Leeds goals: 35.
Scotland: 32 caps, 1 goal.
Other clubs: Nottingham Forest, Sunderland, Darlington.

Dynam

LUCAS RADEBE

'The Chief' was one of the most popular defenders and captains the club has had. Nelson Mandela said of him: "This is my hero". Began his career as a goalkeeper in South Africa before switching to midfield and then central defence.

Date of birth: April 12, 1969.
Place of birth: Soweto, South Africa.
Leeds career: 1994-2005.
Leeds appearances: 262.
Leeds goals: 3.
South Africa: 70 caps, 2 goals.
Other clubs: ICL Birds, Kaizer Chiefs.

GARY KELLY

Right-back Gary was the only Leeds player outside the Revie era to make over 500 appearances for the club,

Date of birth: July 9, 1974.
Place of birth: Drogheda, Ireland.
Leeds career: 1992-2007.
Leeds appearances: 528
Leeds goals: 4.
Republic of Ireland: 51 caps, 2 goals.
Other clubs: Drogheda United, Home Farm.

NORMAN HUNTER

Nicknamed 'Bites Yer Legs' for his fierce defending, Norman formed a rock-like barrier with Jack Charlton at the heart of Leeds' rearguard in Don Revie's 'Super Leeds' side. One of the best left-footed defenders the game has seen.

Date of birth: October 29, 1943.
Place of birth: Gateshead.
Leeds career: 1962-76.
Leeds appearances: 724.
Leeds goals: 21.
England: 28 caps, 2 goals.
Other clubs: Bristol City, Barnsley.

Nicknamed 'Zico'. Often charged forward from right-back to fire in thunderous shots at goal.

Date of birth: October 1, 1961.
Place of birth: Sheffield.
Leeds career: 1989-94.
Leeds appearances: 147.
Leeds goals: 20.
England: 1 cap, no goals.
Other clubs: Sheffield Wednesday, Rangers, Boston United.

MEL STERLAND

Defenders

JONATHAN WOODGATE

The central defender came through Leeds' youth system to gain England honours before joining Newcastle for £9million in January, 2003.

Date of birth: January 22, 1980.
Place of birth: Middlesbrough.
Leeds career: 1996-2003.
Leeds appearances: 141.
Leeds goals: 4.
England: 8 caps, 0 goals.
Other clubs: Middlesbrough, Newcastle United, Real Madrid, Tottenham Hotspur, Stoke City.

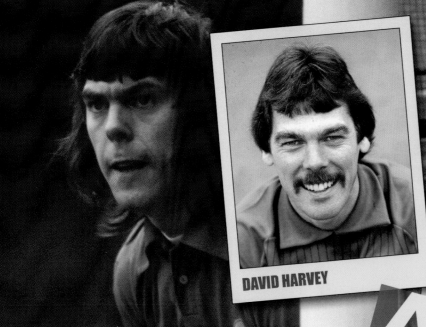

DAVID HARVEY

Leeds' keeper when they won the FA Cup against Arsenal in 1972. Became first choice ahead of Gary Sprake. Had three spells at the club and won a League Championship medal in 1974.

Date of birth: February 7, 1948.
Place of birth: Leeds.
Leeds career: 1965-80, 1980-81 and 1982-85.
Leeds appearances: 446.
Scotland: 16 caps.
Other clubs: Vancouver Whitecaps, Partick Thistle, Bradford City, Whitby Town, Morton, Harrogate Town.

Agile

MERVYN DAY

Won promotion with Leeds from Division Two in 1990. At 19 became the youngest keeper to play in an FA Cup Final when West Ham defeated Fulham in 1975.

Date of birth: June 26, 1955.
Place of birth: Chelmsford.
Leeds career: 1985-93.
Leeds appearances: 265.
Other clubs: West Ham United, Leyton Orient, Aston Villa, Luton Town (loan), Sheffield United (loan), Carlisle United.

PAUL ROBINSON

Famously headed a goal in a home Carling Cup second round tie against Swindon Town in September, 2003, taking the tie into extra time. Excellent shot-stopper who succeeded Nigel Martyn at Leeds and was sold to Tottenham for £1.5million in May, 2004. Retired from international football with England in 2010.

Date of birth: October 15, 1979.
Place of birth: Beverley.
Leeds career: 1998-2004.
Leeds appearances: 119, 1 goal.
England: 41 caps.
Other clubs: York City, Tottenham Hotspur, Blackburn Rovers.

GARY SPRAKE

Don Revie's first choice keeper for many years. Brilliant on his day but tended to make mistakes on big occasions.

Date of birth: April 3, 1945.
Place of birth: Swansea.
Leeds career: 1962-73.
Leeds appearances: 506.
Wales: 37 caps.
Other clubs: Birmingham City.

JOHN LUKIC

Won league titles at Leeds and Arsenal, his only two clubs. Played at the highest level of English league football in four decades.

Date of birth: December 11, 1960.
Place of birth: Chesterfield.
Leeds career: 1978-83, 1990-96.
Leeds appearances: 430.
Other clubs: Arsenal.

Keepers

NIGEL MARTYN

Voted by Leeds fans the club's greatest ever keeper. When Howard Wilkinson bought him from Crystal Palace in 1996 the Leeds manager paid a then record £2.25m fee for a keeper.

Date of birth: August 11, 1966.
Place of birth: St Austell.
Leeds career: 1996-2003.
Leeds appearances: 273.
England: 23 caps.
Other clubs: Bristol Rovers, Crystal Palace, Everton.

Day in the life of a first team wannabe

PROMISING centre-back Afolabi Coker is the envy of his pals. As a Leeds United trainee, the South East Londoner was part of Richard Naylor's Under-18 squad which won their league last May.

Now in his second year at the club and armed with a one-year professional contract, he arrives at work every day with a spring in his step, determined to carve out a successful career and describing this as "a make or break year."

But what's it like to be one of the many youngsters looking to impress United's coaches enough to progress all the way into the first team? Afolabi, 18, is out of bed early, even though training sessions don't start until 10.30am and last until about noon. It's a healthy lunch menu at Thorp Arch, tailored to athletes, and the gym is an important place as the players work on their physical fitness.

"The training sessions are very varied," says Afolabi. "Some days we do running and a bit of football and some days it's all football. We have a double session on Tuesdays and the second session sees the defenders, midfielders and forwards splitting into their own groups, working on their specialist positions and skills.

"Richard Naylor has helped me a lot because he was a centre-half and we work on things like positioning, reading the game and anticipation. We finish between 3.30pm and 4pm and by then we're absolutely shattered so I just sleep or play on the Xbox.

"Training is hard work but it's very enjoyable. There's plenty of banter between the lads too. It's important that we all get on well. When I first came north I couldn't really understand everyone, but I've got used to it now and I understand the jokes!"

Trainees receive core skills lessons, ranging from the rules of the game to financial advice, and they carry on their education in chosen subjects so they have something to fall back on in case their dream of making a living from football falls through.

Afolabi started out as a left back but soon moved to centre-back and sees that as his specialist position now. He has the confidence in his ability that all youngsters need to succeed and the upheaval of leaving home was softened by the presence of close friend Smith Tiesse, a left back who made the same move from South East London and has also landed a one-year professional contract.

So how did Afolabi first come to United's attention? "My agent brought me here for a trial," he recalled. "Naturally I was nervous but excited at the same time, especially when I was taken on.

"My advice to any young player hoping to become a trainee at a club like Leeds United is to work very hard and hope to get scouted. I was a bit different because, as I said, my agent brought me here for that trial. It's a way of life I could really recommend. The facilities and standard of coaching at Thorp Arch give you every chance to succeed and when you look at the number of players who have made it through the Academy into the first team it's very encouraging.

"My aim now is to push on and get better every day. I played one game for the Under 21s last season and was on their bench a lot. Hopefully I'll play more games for the Under 21s this season. Eventually I hope to make it into the first team and become the best I can be."

Naylor, who guided the Under 18s to glory in his first season as a coach, says: "There is a history of the club producing players and that is something that has been focussed on in recent years. Afolabi and Smith have fully deserved their first professional contracts."

QUESTION AND ANSWER
Noel hunting
for a second promotion

NOEL HUNT knows what it takes to win promotion from the Championship after doing just that under Brian McDermott's management at Reading. Among other topics, we asked him about the career that took him to Elland Road via Shamrock Rovers, Waterford United, Dunfermline, Dundee United and Reading. And he warns that it will take 'blood, sweat and tears' to achieve his big ambition and bring Premier League football back to Leeds United.

Question: Can Brian McDermott get Leeds into the Premier League?
Answer: A definite yes. I wouldn't be here if I thought otherwise. You only need to look at the success he had at Reading.

Q: Was he the main reason you came to Leeds?
A: It was one of the main reasons. The second was the massive response I got off Twitter from the Leeds fans. It made the choice very easy for me. I am close friends with Hartey (Ian Harte) and he told me how brilliant the fans are. They are the driving force behind the 'big steam engine'.

Q: What are Brian's qualities?
A: He's honest and kind. He keeps things simple and is a very calm individual who is so good at what he does. He's a good man-manager who has done so much for me in my career. If you ask him a question and he doesn't know the answer he'll find out and come back to you.

Q: How did you get started at Dunfermline and then Dundee United?
A: I played for Shamrock Rovers in Ireland, left my home town Waterford, came back on loan and had a good friend in Gary Dempsey at Waterford United. He had an outstanding season and was bought by Jimmy Calderwood at Dunfermline.

Gary recommended me, and Jimmy came to watch me at Shamrock Rovers the next season. I went there for a week but he sent me home after three days and said they wanted to sign me in the January. I played there for three years with a lot of good players. Craig Brewster, who was a fine player, left Dunfermline in my third season to become Dundee United's manager so he asked me at the end of the season to go and play for them and I said I would love to. I had two great years there. It was a fantastic club run by very good people.

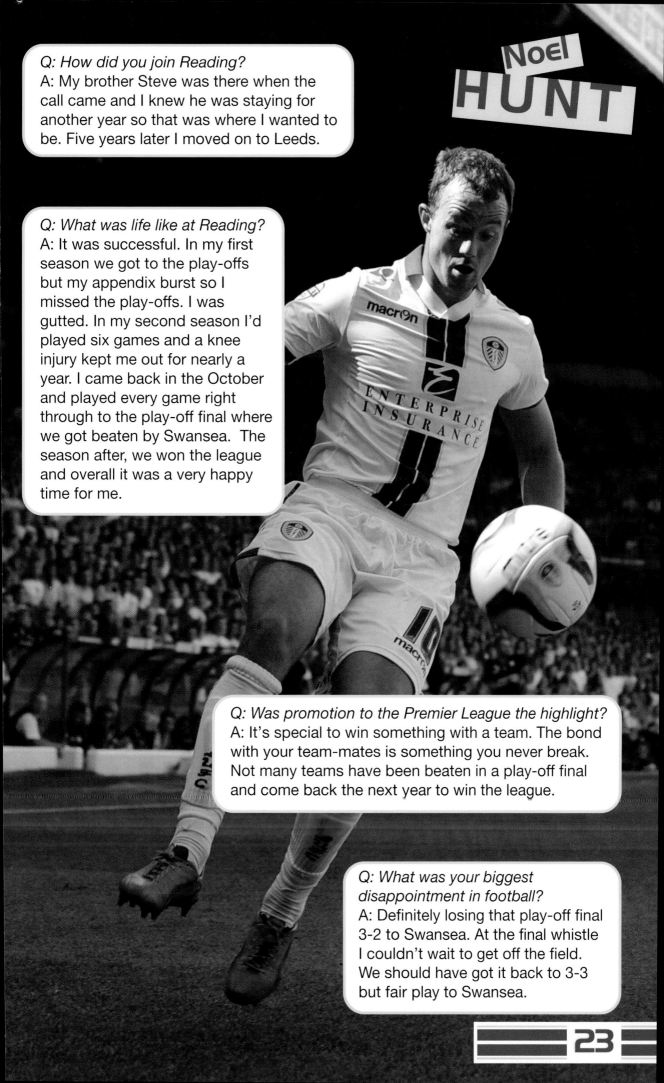

Noel **HUNT**

Q: How did you join Reading?
A: My brother Steve was there when the call came and I knew he was staying for another year so that was where I wanted to be. Five years later I moved on to Leeds.

Q: What was life like at Reading?
A: It was successful. In my first season we got to the play-offs but my appendix burst so I missed the play-offs. I was gutted. In my second season I'd played six games and a knee injury kept me out for nearly a year. I came back in the October and played every game right through to the play-off final where we got beaten by Swansea. The season after, we won the league and overall it was a very happy time for me.

Q: Was promotion to the Premier League the highlight?
A: It's special to win something with a team. The bond with your team-mates is something you never break. Not many teams have been beaten in a play-off final and come back the next year to win the league.

Q: What was your biggest disappointment in football?
A: Definitely losing that play-off final 3-2 to Swansea. At the final whistle I couldn't wait to get off the field. We should have got it back to 3-3 but fair play to Swansea.

23

Q: Who is the best player you've played with and against?
A: I played with Paul McGrath in a testimonial in Ireland many years ago. I must have been 21. I've played with some great players but he was my hero as a kid. Cannavaro is the best player I've played against, in the World Cup qualifiers. He was superb.

Q: Do you carry any grudges into matches against certain players?
A: No. You can't do that. The game is too important to worry about one individual. If you allow yourself to be wound up by an individual it takes your mind-set off the game and that affects the team.

Q: What advice would you give to a young player just starting out?
A: Listen to the older players, your coaches and manager and do what they say. Cut out the negative influences and concentrate on the positives. Always do what is best for the team. The more you learn, the more you earn. That's what I've always been taught.

Q: What is your match-day routine?
A: I'm out of bed by quarter-to-nine, breakfast, back to bed at half past nine, up at eleven, shower, suit, pre-match, game. That's it. Nothing too complicated.

Q: What are your biggest likes and dislikes about football?
A: Winning is my biggest like. I don't care who scores the goals because it's a team game. Being out injured is my biggest dislike. Long term injuries are horrible and I've had two of them. I broke my ankle when I was 21 and that knee injury at Reading was very frustrating. It's no fun when your team-mates are playing and you're not, but I could have been stuck in an office with a broken ankle or a bad knee. I'm so thankful that I'm a footballer.

Q: What is your biggest ambition in football?
A: To get promoted again. We have to earn it because it's not going to be a walk in the park. It's a big ask and a big challenge but I am confident we can do it. It will take blood, sweat and tears. They reckon this is the hardest league in the world to get out of and I would agree.

Q: Do you have any superstitions?
A: Yes. When putting on my kit before a game I always put everything on the right side first – the right sock, the right boot etc. I even put my right foot in my shorts first! My right foot is my strongest.

Q: Do you set yourself a goals target every season?
A: Yes. Realistically I like to get into double figures before the middle of January, though I'm not disappointed if I fall short of that if the team are doing well. If we are not doing well, I'll have a look at myself.

Q: What is your favourite position in the team?
A: Striker. I like playing up front and making runs for my fellow strikers. If they do the same for me, that's fine. I've known some players who are selfish and it doesn't work. I'll work my socks off for my team-mate and I expect him to do the same. That's how it should be.

Q: Did you start out as a striker?
A: No. I was a goalkeeper. I went on trial to Crystal Palace as a goalkeeper but was told I was too small. We had too many keepers training one day so I went downfield and I remember scoring a few goals – nothing special. Then match-day came and I wasn't in goal so I thought I'd been dropped. I played right wing and then up-front, we won 4-2 and I scored all four goals, so it all happened from there.

Q: Who do you most admire in football and why?
A: My older brother Steve. He was always playing leagues ahead of me so I was always trying to catch him up. We played together for a year at Reading and that was special.

Q: Favourite holiday destination?
A: I went to St Lucia in the summer and it was beautiful, so peaceful and quiet.

Q: What is your favourite food and is it healthy?
A: I do eat healthy food – a lot of veg and meat. I like a burger once a month, but that's all.

Q: If you could have one wish in the world what would it be?
A: Health and happiness for a long time.

Q: Main interests outside football?
A: I like a bit of golf. I'm horrendous but I love it. No-one ever masters it. I love the sport of hurling back home in Ireland too.

Q: If you hadn't been a footballer what would you have been?
A: I would probably have gone into coaching. That is something I fancy when I stop playing. I like to think I am a good influence and have a good input.

Making sure they're fit to wear the white shirt

Matt Pears, Leeds United's fitness conditioning coach, has one of the most important roles at the club.

The modern game is played with such pace and power that players have to be in peak physical condition if they are to cope with the demands on their bodies, both during matches and in training.

Matt, who studied for a Masters in Sport and Exercise Science at Leeds Met, says that even school kids who are just starting to learn the game have a whole host of things they can do to make sure they are better prepared to play. "Firstly they need to be comfortable using both feet," Matt says. "There are a lot of footwork drills that can be done.

"Also it's important to run through some exercises in the gym. Even players aged 11 to 14 can start improving lower body strength and some upper body strength, but they must be supervised. Ideally, seek out a fitness coach at your club or seek advice. Most gyms run programmes that have fitness coaches for all age groups because it is important to be supervised by qualified professionals.

"Progressing to the older age groups we load up exercises such as single leg squats, split squats and lunges. We work on the typical areas where players pick up injuries, such as hamstrings, calves and ankles. We have to make sure hamstring and calf muscles are as strong and robust as possible because a first team player could play upwards of 60 games a season.

"We want the manager to be able to select from his best players, week in, week out, so if players have strong muscles and joints they can withstand the regular 90 minutes football and all the training.

"If muscles and joints are weak they break down and injuries can cost a scholar, for instance, the opportunity to showcase himself. "

Matt says there is a big debate going on about what age fitness conditioning should start, but body weight exercises at even low level strength, using medicine balls for instance, can be beneficial from age 11 onwards. He says: "It has been shown that if we never even trained the young Academy players, their path of development would improve because they are growing, but we can speed that up by using strength training."

Matt enjoys working with the first team squad and the other age groups at the club and says first team squad members just need fine tuning. "No two players respond the same to a training programme or require exactly the same programme," he added. "Paul Green is a very good all-round athlete. He ticks all the boxes because he has speed and a very good engine. He just keeps going and going.

"Dominic Poleon is one of the quickest we've had through the doors but he still needed to work on aspects of his fitness. Sometimes players have the mentality that they are fit enough or quick enough, but they need to ask themselves: am I the fittest I can be? There is always something you can improve upon."

Sam scoops up awards galore

By any standards, Sam Byram's debut season was a rip-roaring success. The young right back carried off so many awards that his mantle-piece must have buckled under the weight.

Yet Leeds United's Player of the Year is one of the most modest people you could wish to meet and is grateful to the coaching staff who improved his already considerable ability as he progressed through the club's Academy and Under 21s into the first team.

Sam was only denied an ever-present first season of Championship football by a hip injury collected in the warm-up to the final home game of the 2012-13 campaign against Brighton, which also caused him to miss the last match of the season, at Watford, withdraw from the England squad for the FIFA Under 20 World Cup in Turkey and miss the start of the 2013-14 campaign.

The England blow was especially disappointing, but if Sam continues to maintain his rapid rate of progress there are sure to be many international opportunities coming his way.

Looking back on his excellent first season, Sam said: "It has been a whirlwind year, from going to Cornwall with the first team in pre-season to standing here now after playing all those games. I am really delighted and proud how things have gone – apart from the injury, of course.

"I never expected to play so many games but Neil Warnock showed his faith in me. I think I did a good job for him and hopefully I can do the same for the new manager, Brian McDermott. After pre-season I would have been happy going back into the Under 21s and taking my time trying to break into the first team, but it all happened so fast – brilliant!"

Sam, who made his senior debut in the 4-0 Capital One Cup win over Shrewsbury Town, on August 11, 2012, was handed his league bow seven days later in a 1-0 home win against Wolves, making 53 consecutive appearances in all competitions before that pre-match hip injury in late April.

He said: "Someone spoke to me the year before my debut suggesting I might have got on to the bench but I had broken my toe, so that put me out for the end of that season. It left me keen to get fully fit again and as close to a first team place as possible.

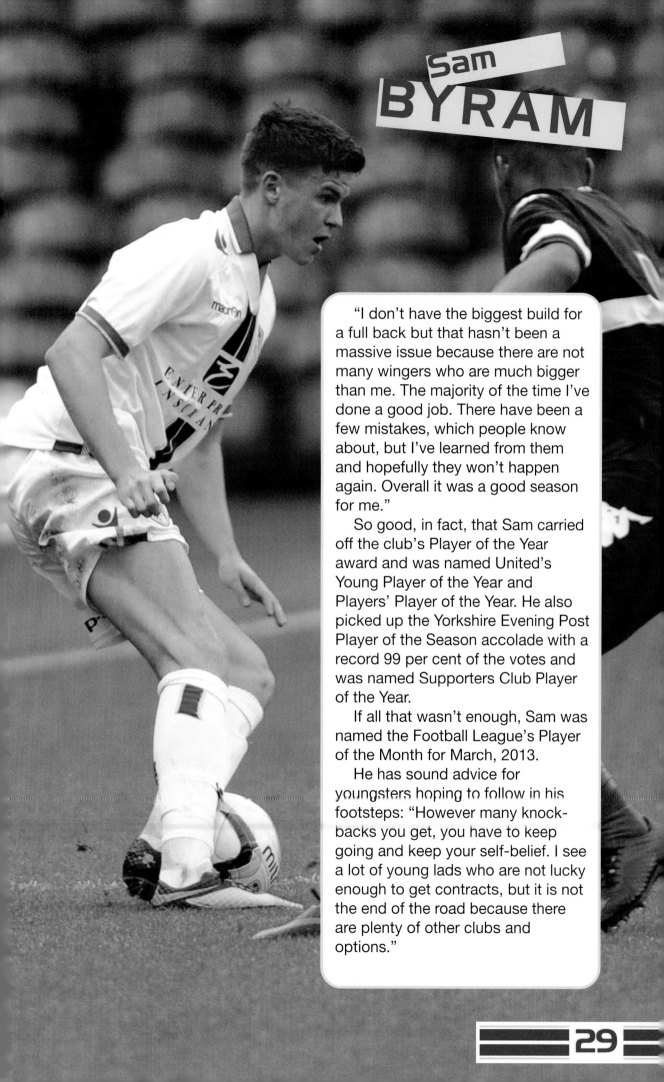

"I don't have the biggest build for a full back but that hasn't been a massive issue because there are not many wingers who are much bigger than me. The majority of the time I've done a good job. There have been a few mistakes, which people know about, but I've learned from them and hopefully they won't happen again. Overall it was a good season for me."

So good, in fact, that Sam carried off the club's Player of the Year award and was named United's Young Player of the Year and Players' Player of the Year. He also picked up the Yorkshire Evening Post Player of the Season accolade with a record 99 per cent of the votes and was named Supporters Club Player of the Year.

If all that wasn't enough, Sam was named the Football League's Player of the Month for March, 2013.

He has sound advice for youngsters hoping to follow in his footsteps: "However many knock-backs you get, you have to keep going and keep your self-belief. I see a lot of young lads who are not lucky enough to get contracts, but it is not the end of the road because there are plenty of other clubs and options."

Leeds United have had many different kits over the years. Don Revie famously changed the team's colours to all-white like Real Madrid. We think the present-day kit is ace but what are your favourites? Here are some of the kits that have been worn by United. You can vote them a hit or miss in the circles provided.

United promote a healthy lifestyle for schoolchildren

BRIAN McDermott was quick to stress the importance of youth after he became Leeds United's manager.

Successive wins against Sheffield Wednesday and Burnley in April ended any fears of relegation from the Championship, but less than 24 hours after the victory over the Clarets, McDermott was busy encouraging pupils at a local primary school to take up football, spend less time on their PlayStations and enjoy a healthy lifestyle.

United are spending £100,000 on a scheme to give five to 11-year-olds across the city access to football coaching and other healthy activities.

And former Reading manager McDermott joined members of the coaching staff and players Ross McCormack, Sam Byram and Tom Lees on a visit to Clapgate Primary School, Belle Isle, to launch the scheme.

He explained: "We never had footballers coming into schools when I was young – which was a long time ago! I started a Football in the Community scheme from scratch when I stopped playing at Slough and I really enjoyed working with the kids.

"I was asked to set up the scheme back then. I didn't have a clue what I was doing at first so I just made it up as I went along, but we finally got to where we wanted to be and it was a very rewarding experience. The kids love it when the people from their local club come in, coach them and give advice.

"It's not about trying to find elite players. It's more about getting everybody playing football and enjoying themselves. Sometimes talent is discovered from that, but it's not the main reason for the scheme."

McDermott is impressed by the youngsters coming through at Leeds. First team regulars Byram and Lees attended the club's Academy and one of McDermott's early decisions was to promote Development Squad Manager Neil Redfearn to coach the first team and Under 21s.

McDermott said: "I've known Neil for a long time. Coaching the first team and looking after the Under 21s is a really good combination. I am encouraged by the standard of the staff here and the young talent coming through."

Name their countries

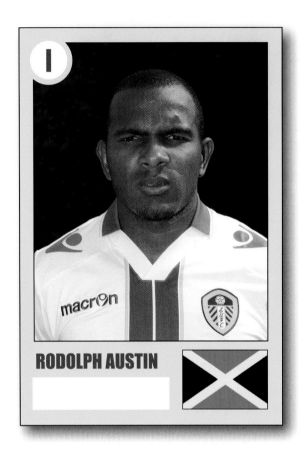

1

RODOLPH AUSTIN

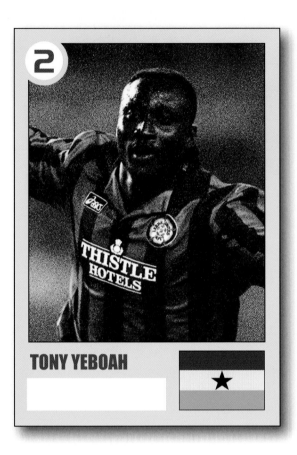

2

TONY YEBOAH

3

ROSS McCORMACK

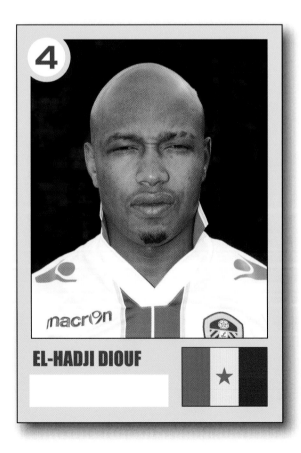

4

EL-HADJI DIOUF

Here are eight past or present Leeds United players. Can you name the countries they've played for? As a clue we've accompanied each player's name and picture with the flag of his country. The answers are on Page 63.

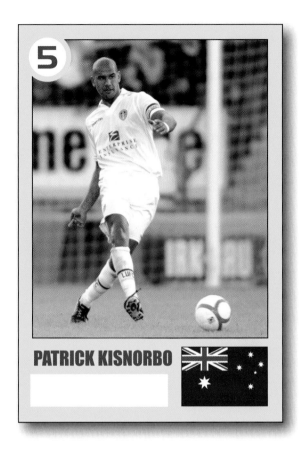

5

PATRICK KISNORBO

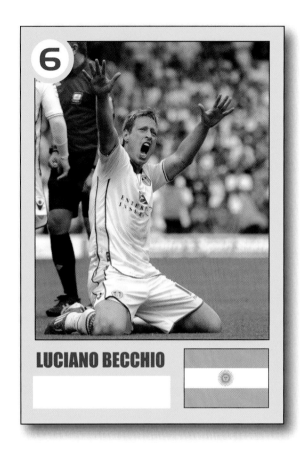

6

LUCIANO BECCHIO

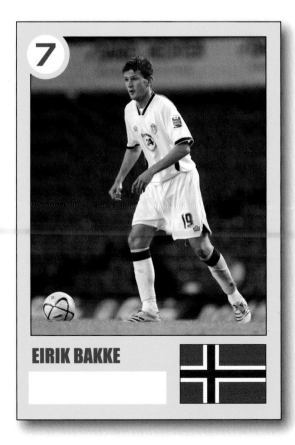

7

EIRIK BAKKE

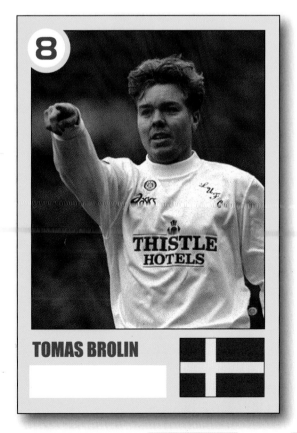

8

TOMAS BROLIN

Summing up the squad numbers

Here's a teaser to test your maths and get you familiar with the players' squad numbers.

1. MATT SMITH + LUKE MURPHY =

2. PAUL GREEN X LEE PELTIER =

3. MICHAEL TONGE ÷ ADAM DRURY =

4. SAM BYRAM - AIDY WHITE =

SQUAD NUMBERS: 1 PADDY KENNY, 2 LEE PELTIER, 3 ADAM DRURY, 4 TOM LEES, 5 JASON PEARCE, 6 LUKE MURPHY, 7 PAUL GREEN, 8 RODOLPH AUSTIN, 10 NOEL HUNT, 11 LUKE VARNEY, 12 JAMIE ASHDOWN, 14 AIDY WHITE, 15 STEPHEN WARNOCK 16 DANNY PUGH, 17 MICHAEL BROWN, 18 MICHAEL TONGE

Using the squad numbers, can you work out these 8 simple sums?
For instance, Noel Hunt wears squad number 10 and Luke Varney wears number 11.
Add them together and your answer is 21.

5 JAMIE ASHDOWN + EL-HADJI DIOUF =

6 ROSS McCORMACK − NOEL HUNT =

7 LUKE VARNEY X TOM LEES =

8 STEPHEN WARNOCK ÷ JASON PEARCE =

19 DAVID NORRIS , 20 MATT SMITH, 21 EL-HADJI DIOUF, 22 SCOTT WOOTTON, 23 ZAC THOMPSON, 25 SAM BYRAM, 26 DOMINIC POLEON, 29 SIMON LENIGHAN, 30 RYAN HALL, 31 CHARLIE TAYLOR, 32 CHRIS DAWSON, 33 ALEX CAIRNS, 34 ROSS KILLOCK, 44 ROSS McCORMACK.

England, Scotland or France for our Matt?

If Matt Smith reaches international standard he could have three countries battling for his services.

For Leeds United's 6ft 6in striker qualifies to play for England, Scotland and France. Matt, 24, is the first to admit he is not yet the finished article, after being a late entrant to full time football, but he has the confidence and ambition to go right to the top.

Although Matt was born in Birmingham, his father Ian is a Scot, who played for Hearts and Birmingham City, and Matt's grandfather also played professional football. The French connection comes from relatives on his mother's side but they died before he was born.

During his non-League days, Matt was called up for the England C squad, though he says: "If I do go on to play full international football, there are options because I have English, Scottish and French in me. Playing for England would be the highest honour but my dad won a few amateur caps in Scotland so to be able to follow in his footsteps and play for Scotland would be an appealing route I could possibly take."

Matt, who joined the club from Oldham in the summer, is quick to point out that holding down a first team place at Elland Road and improving as a player are his top priorities and adds: "I have the facilities, the coaching and the players around me to come on by leaps and bounds, so it's an exciting prospect.

"I am here to play – not to make up the numbers - and I want to be a regular part of the team, not just the squad. It is up to me to prove myself and do well."

He played non-league football for Cheltenham Town, Redditch United, Droylsden and Solihull Moors before Oldham manager Paul Dickov gave him his first chance in full time football – something for which Matt will always be grateful. This is only his third full season of league combat but he believes starting out in non-league has helped him appreciate life as a full-time pro and kept his feet on the ground.

"Coming from non-league is different, but playing at that level got me into first team football much quicker than if I had joined a league club's academy and worked my way up through the reserves," he said. "It toughens you up from an earlier age too. I was still filling out at 17 or 18 years old so I grew up pretty quickly and was able to rise up the ladder."

Brainbox Matt combined playing non-league with studying international business management, spending three years at Manchester University and one year in Arizona, America. To help fund his studies he boosted his income from non-league football by working in a hotel, doing bar work and waiting at tables, along with other jobs here and there.

"Looking back, doing those jobs has helped me realise how blessed I am to be a full time footballer," said Matt. "You can't beat being paid to keep fit and do something you love. The studies mean I have something to fall back on, but I've said from the first day I joined Oldham that I want to give my football career a real go."

Highlights of his time with Oldham were the goals he scored in the FA Cup against Liverpool and Everton, being named Player of the FA Cup fifth round and picking up the Player of the Month award for April.

"The goals earned the club a lot of money but I didn't want to be simply known as the guy who scored those FA Cup goals," said Matt. "I wanted to back it up with some league form, which I was happy to do, and we survived a relegation dogfight.

"My first season at Oldham was one of slow progress, as I was finding my feet in full time football, but I had a great back-end to my second season and scored those four goals against Premier League opposition. After two years in League One and now in my first season in the Championship I want to keep going onwards and upwards."

2012-13

IT WAS a case of out with the old, in with the new, as manager Neil Warnock attempted an outright record eighth promotion in his long career, but a much changed team failed to deliver a ticket back into the Premiership.

Warnock left after a 2-1 home defeat to Derby County on April 1, 2013, with the club in 12th place, eight points off the play-offs and just five above the relegation zone.

Neil Redfearn was placed in temporary charge, just as he had been when Simon Grayson lost his job in February, 2012, but Redfearn didn't want the job permanently and the arrival of former Reading manager Brian McDermott, who signed a three-year-contract, filled supporters with fresh hope.

McDermott's appointment, with five matches of the season remaining, came too late to have much impact on the 2012-13 season, but relegation was avoided and United finished 13th with 61 points – exactly the tally they had gathered a year earlier when they finished 14th.

August

Unusually, the season began with the Capital One Cup first round, and a Leeds team containing ten debutants (Paddy Kenny, Lee Peltier, Jason Pearce, Paul Green, Rodolph Austin, Luke Varney, David Norris, Sam Byram and substitutes El-Hadji Diouf and Dominic Poleon) swept aside visitors Shrewsbury Town 4-0 with goals by Luciano Becchio, Luke Varney, David Norris and Ross McCormack.

The opening league game, against Wolves at Elland Road, was televised live by Sky, and Luciano Becchio's diving header earned United a 1-0 win. However, the first defeat of the campaign came just three days later at Blackpool where Tom Lees nodded the Whites into a 17th minute lead, only for the Tangerines to score two late goals.

El-Hadji Diouf and Adam Drury made their first starts in a 2-1 win at Peterborough where there were also league debuts for substitutes Andy Gray (in his second spell at the club) and Dominic Poleon. Luciano Becchio scored both goals.

Oxford United suffered a 3-0 Capital One Cup defeat at Elland Road with Rodolph Austin and Sam Byram grabbing their first goals for the Whites in spectacular fashion and Tom Lees heading the third.

September

Blackburn, unbeaten in the league, were the next visitors, United hitting back from two down to lead 3-2 before drawing 3-3. El-Hadji Diouf scored his first goal for the club but missed a sitter against one of his former teams, deep into added time.

United went to Cardiff without a win in Wales since 1984 and there was more bad news as they lost 2-1 and had Ross McCormack carried off with an ankle injury. Rodolph Austin's first league goal was struck from 30 yards.

Hull City gained their first win at Elland Road for 25 years as United went down 3-2. Andy Gray headed his first goal since returning to the club and Luciano Becchio's penalty was lucky after El-Hadji Diouf had been fouled just outside the box.

Dominic Poleon will long remember September 22, 2013. He made his first start and scored his first goal in a 2-1 home win over Nottingham Forest, after Luciano Becchio had opened the scoring. It was Aidy White's turn to score his maiden goal for the club when Everton were beaten 2-1 at Elland Road in the Capital One Cup third round in front of the Sky cameras. Everton were lying third in the Premiership and Neil Warnock described the result as his best in the competition. Rodolph Austin was also on target.

September ended with a third successive victory. Michael Tonge's goal in a 3-2 success at Bristol City was his first for anyone since December, 2010, and El-Hadji-Diouf scored twice.

October

United's first visit to the Reebok Stadium ended in a 2-2 draw, two headers by Kevin Davies from corners denying Warnock's men victory. El-Hadji-Diouf captained the side against another of his old clubs and hit the bar in time added on. Sam Byram headed his first league goal and Luciano Becchio's penalty brought his eighth goal of the season. Becchio was on target from the spot again, with a cheeky chip into the middle of the goal, to settle the Yorkshire derby against Barnsley.

Michael Tonge's sweetly struck equaliser earned a 1-1 draw at Sheffield Wednesday. Another 1-1 draw, at home to Charlton, made it seven games without defeat but Warnock described his team as "plodders". David Norris's goal was his first for the club.

The unbeaten run ended with a 1-0 home defeat against Birmingham whose manager Lee Clark was celebrating his 40th birthday. Ryan Hall left the bench for his Leeds debut. October ended on a high with a 3-0 home triumph over Premiership side Southampton in the Capital One Cup fourth round as United reached the quarter-finals for the first time since 1996. Luciano Becchio tucked away a penalty in injury-time, a minute after leaving the bench. Michael Tonge and El-Hadji Diouf were the other scorers.

November

United fans faced the long trip to Gus Poyet's Brighton on a Friday night and twice hit back to force a 2-2 draw. Michael Brown scored his only goal of the season, El-Hadji Diouf netted from the penalty spot and Paddy Kenny saved a penalty but Craig Mackail-Smith scored twice for Brighton.

Burnley gained their first win over Leeds since 2006 with Charlie Austin's 20th goal of the season, at Turf Moor, but worse was to follow with a 6-1 home thrashing against Watford. United finished the game with nine men after Jason Pearce was sent off and Rodolph Austin was carried off with a cracked ankle bone. It became seven league games without a win as United lost 1-0 at Millwall where Luke Varney was sent off and Ross McCormack made his comeback after injury. The Lions won it with an 85th minute header from substitute Chris Wood.

New owners GFH Capital saw United defeat league leaders Crystal Palace 2-1 at Elland Road to end seven league games without a win. Loan players Jerome Thomas and Alan Tate made their debuts. Palace had gone 14 matches unbeaten but goals from Luciano Becchio and Paul Green won it for Leeds.

A 1-0 home win over Leicester gave United back-to-back victories for the first time since September, Luciano Becchio's penalty coming after only three minutes. It was the Whites' first Tuesday night home league win since August, 2011.

December

The West Yorkshire derby at Huddersfield saw United gain a 4-2 victory for their first win over the Terriers in six attempts. Luciano Becchio's two goals took his tally for the season to 14 and the other Leeds scorers were David Norris and Michael Tonge. Chris Atkinson had given Town an early lead and Adam Clayton scored from the penalty spot for the Terriers against his old club.

The joy of beating Huddersfield quickly gave way to disappointment with a 3-1 reverse at Derby where Paul Green was made captain and scored against his former team. Green was again on the mark, along with Jerome Thomas, in a 2-0 home win against Ipswich but United's Capital One Cup run ended with a 5-1 defeat by Chelsea at Elland Road. Luciano Becchio put Leeds a goal up but Chelsea's Premiership pedigree told in the second half.

Leading scorer Becchio took his goals total to 17 for the season and seven in seven games with a brace in a 2-1 home win over Middlesbrough, but a 4-2 defeat followed at Nottingham Forest on Boxing Day. Substitute Davide Somma scored his first goal for the Whites since a long spell out injured and Paul Green also netted for the losers. Forest sacked manager Sean O'Driscoll despite the win.

Somma made his first start for 19 months at Hull where Luciano Becchio was missing with a thigh injury and United ended 2012 with a 2-0 defeat.

January

The new year got off to a winning start with that man Becchio netting his sixth penalty and his 18th goal of the campaign as Bolton were sent home empty-handed. The Argentine then earned United an FA Cup third round replay with an equaliser in a 1-1 draw with Birmingham. Neil Warnock missed the game with a virus but kept in touch by phone and ordered two substitutions at half time, El-Hadji Diouf and Sam Byram replacing Ryan Hall and Aidy White.

Ross Barkley, on loan from Everton, made his debut in a 2-0 league defeat at Barnsley but United went on to win their FA Cup replay at Birmingham 2-1. With Luciano Becchio out through illness, El-Hadji Diouf scored from the spot on his 32nd birthday, to make it ten successful penalties out of ten by United since the season's start. Ross McCormack was also on the mark but Adam Drury suffered an ankle injury which was to keep him out until April.

Bottom of the table Bristol City lost 1-0 at Elland Road with Sean O'Driscoll in charge for the first time, Ross McCormack securing the points with a 66th minute header. United reached the FA Cup fifth round for the first time in ten years with a superb 2-1 home win over Spurs, who were fourth in the Premiership. Luciano Becchio was left out after asking for a transfer but Luke Varney and Ross McCormack saw United through. Becchio duly joined Norwich City on the final day of January for cash, plus Steve Morison.

February

Cardiff arrived at Elland Road as runaway leaders and United failed to score at home for only the second time since the season's start. Fraizer Campbell landed the only goal, two minutes after leaving the bench for his debut after a £650,000 move from Sunderland. Habib Habibou made his Leeds debut, also from the bench. It was the turn of Stephen Warnock and Steve Morison to make their debuts in a 2-2 draw at Wolves where Danny Batth's injury-time headed equaliser denied Neil Warnock's men the points.

Middlesbrough's first win in six league games saw goal-scorer Curtis Main sent off for two bookable offences at the Riverside. United's FA Cup run ended with a 4-0 defeat at Manchester City who were two up in the opening 15 minutes.

David Norris and Steve Morison, with his first goal for the club, steadied things with a 2-0 home win against Blackpool for whom Paul Ince made a losing start to his spell in charge. United kept their first away clean sheet of the season in a goalless draw at Blackburn to leave them six points off the top six.

March

Ross McCormack had a 12th minute penalty saved against Millwall at Elland Road, but Stephen Warnock took over the role to score his first goal for the club, in the 72nd minute, and it proved to be the winner. Sam Byram must have thought his goal at Leicester was going to earn the points until Michael Keane came along with an injury-time headed equaliser for the Foxes.

Steve Morison netted twice for Leeds and Glenn Murray twice for Crystal Palace in a 2-2 draw at Selhurst Park and Sam Byram rescued a home point after Dwight Gayle had opened the scoring for lowly Peterborough at Elland Road. United's 2-1 home defeat to West Yorkshire neighbours Huddersfield Town was described by Neil Warnock as "possibly fatal" in the bid for the play-offs. Aidy White's header was his first league goal for Leeds and came two minutes after he left the bench.

United ended the month with a disappointing 3-0 result at Ipswich Town in a game that saw Tom Lees receive his marching orders in the first half.

April

Warnock ended his reign in charge after a 2-1 home defeat against Derby in which Chris Dawson made his debut, aged 18. It was United's third successive league loss and their sixth game without a win. They were eight points off the play-offs and five above the relegation zone.

United went to Charlton with Neil Redfearn in temporary charge and Richard Naylor lending assistance but came away beaten 2-1, substitute Jonathan Obika's cruel winner arriving four minutes into time added on.

Brian McDermott received a warm welcome from Leeds fans when he took charge of the team for the first time against Sheffield Wednesday at Elland Road on April 13. A crowd of 23,936 turned up and saw two second half headers by Luke Varney from Ross McCormack's pinpoint crosses ensure McDermott's reign got off to a winning start after Jermaine Johnson had given Wednesday a 27th minute lead.

When Burnley arrived at Elland Road three days later, the crowd dipped by more than 7,000 but Rodolph Austin's first goal since September made it two wins out of two for McDermott. The side's first defeat under McDermott arrived at Birmingham, where Hayden Mullins' 71st minute goal separated the teams, and the last home game of the season, against Brighton, proved eventful, to say the least.

Brighton's 2-1 win ensured their place in the play-offs, but Leeds finished with nine men against Brighton's ten after dismissals for Rodolph Austin, El-Hadji-Diouf and Inigo Calderon.

May

A season of so many disappointments finished on a winning note at Watford whose ten men needed a win for automatic promotion after Hull drew with Cardiff. Dominic Poleon's first goal since his recall from Sheffield United was the first to be scored in the first half by a Leeds player in 22 league games!

An incredible 16 minutes had to be added to the first half after injuries to Leeds' Steve Morison and Watford's stand-in keeper Jonathan Bond, who was himself replaced by debutant Jack Bonham, 19. Almen Abdi equalised six minutes into time added on in the first half, Watford's Troy Deeney was sent off in the 61st minute for a second bookable offence and Ross McCormack's late lob won it for the Whites.

Have you been paying attention?

ONE of our most popular features in the past has been a quiz to see how much knowledge you've gained from reading the Leeds United Annual. Here are this year's 10 questions and some pictures to help you work out the answers, which are on page 63.

1 Which Leeds United player missed only two matches in the 2012-13 season?

2 Who was placed in temporary charge after manager Neil Warnock left the club?

3 Who scored his first goal in his first start during United's 2-1 win against Nottingham Forest in September, 2013?

4 Who scored his only goal of the season in a 2-2 draw at Brighton in November, 2013?

5 Who scored twice for United in the 4-2 West Yorkshire derby win at Huddersfield Town in December, 2013?

6 Which striker scored from the penalty spot on his 32nd birthday in an FA Cup replay victory at Birmingham in January, 2013.

7 Which club did Brian McDermott manage before taking charge at Elland Road?

8 Which countries does Matt Smith qualify to play for?

9 Which two teams did Noel Hunt play for in Scotland?

10 In what position does Leeds youngster Afolabi Coker play?

Paul
GREEN

47

Name that badge!

Footballers love to kiss their club badge after scoring a goal. Can you name the Yorkshire clubs these badges belong to? Answers on Page 63.

1

2

3

4

5 ⬭

6 ⬭

7 ⬭

8 ⬭

9 ⬭

10 ⬭

Mystery Leeds stars

Can you identify these players from Leeds United's past and present? We've given you some clues to help, including the players' initials. The answers are on Page 63.

1 This Liverpool-born defender was named captain for the 2012-13 season. He joined the club from Leicester City and has played for another West Yorkshire club, Huddersfield Town.

L   P

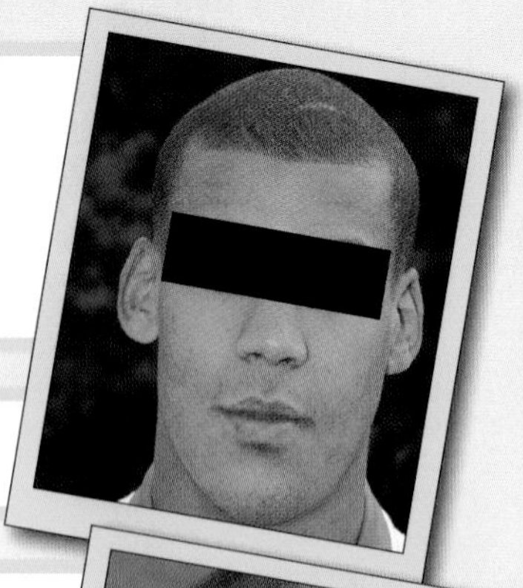

2 A former Leeds United captain and defender who joined from Liverpool in August, 2000, and is an ambassador for the club.

D   M

3 Striker signed from Norwich in part exchange for Luciano Becchio. Joined Millwall on a season-long loan.

S   M

4 Jamaican international midfielder who joined United from Norwegian club SK Brann.

R   A

5 Goalkeeper whose father shone in the same position for Manchester United and Denmark.

K   S

6 Legendary former Leeds and Scotland winger who managed the club in the eighties and had a spell as caretaker-manager after Peter Reid left the club.

E   G

7 Scored the goal against Arsenal that took the FA Cup to Leeds for the first and only time in 1972.

A   C

8 Midfielder born in Pontefract who signed from Derby County in the summer of 2012.

P   G

9 Former Leeds academy player who attended school in Horsforth, was sold to Newcastle for £5million in 2004 and is a full England international.

J   M

10 Halifax-born goalkeeper signed by Neil Warnock from Queens Park Rangers in the summer of 2012.

P   K

11 Leeds-born striker or midfielder who scored against Liverpool on his debut and was eventually sold to Manchester United.

A _____ S

12 Giant centre-half from the Don Revie era. Known as 'The Giraffe'.

J _____ C

13 Another tall player but this time a striker who in the summer of 2013 became Brian McDermott's first signing as Leeds United's manager.

M _____ S

14 United's top scorer in the 2012-13 season with 19 goals – 15 in the league, three in the Capital One Cup and one in the FA Cup.

L _____ B

15 Australian central defender who has been especially unlucky with injuries.

P _____ K

16 Senegalese striker who has played in the Premiership and scored seven goals for United in the 2012-13 season.

E   H   D

17 Irish international right back who had a testimonial at Elland Road and played over 500 games for the club.

G   K

18 Striker who scored against Manchester United in a 1-0 win at Old Trafford in the FA Cup third round on January 3, 2010.

J   B

19 Left back with the same surname as the manager at the time who left Elland Road at the end of the 2012-13 season.

S   W

20 Former Leeds left back who was a team-mate of Noel Hunt's at Reading.

I   H

AFTER three years in League One, Leeds United saw some light at the end of a very long tunnel as they captured promotion back to the Championship in May, 2010.

Manager Simon Grayson had taken Blackpool from League One into the Championship in 2007 and, after Millwall denied United promotion in the 2009 play-offs, Grayson took the Whites up a year later as they captured second place with 86 points.

It was a season of triumph for striker Jermaine Beckford, who finished with 31 goals – 25 of them in the league. Yet it was his goal against Manchester United at Old Trafford in the FA Cup third round that is best remembered by Leeds fans. Beckford's 20th goal of the season made him the first Leeds player to score a winning goal at Old Trafford since Brian Flynn in February, 1981, and the striker's joy came just a few days after he had asked for a transfer!

Leeds lost a replay against Tottenham in the next round, but that win over Manchester United was a massive confidence boost for the main task – promotion to the Championship.

Grayson's men, with Beckford and Luciano Becchio scoring most of the goals, had been in the top two for most of the season, but with the finishing line approaching, they almost capsized with a run of four defeats – against Southampton, Millwall, Norwich and Swindon – before steadying the ship with successive victories against Yeovil, Southend and Carlisle.

The 3-1 victory at Carlisle lifted United back into second place, a point ahead of Millwall. Beckford was dropped to the bench for that game, but two goals from Becchio and one by Max Gradel saw United home. With four matches to go, the tension was at fever pitch and a 3-2 defeat at Gillingham did nothing to steady nerves, manager Grayson describing his side's first half display as "a shambles".

A remarkable match at Elland Road saw MK Dons finish with eight men after receiving three red cards. Luciano Becchio's 13th minute goal was quickly followed by an equaliser from Dean Lewington. Max Gradel restored United's advantage in the 33rd minute but referee Michael Oliver sent off Mathias Doumbe just before half-time, David McCracken in the 85th minute and Peter Leven just before the end.

Jermaine Beckford left the bench with 15 minutes left and after making it 3-1 in the 80th minute he tucked away a penalty to complete an eventful win and leave United still one point ahead of Millwall. The start of May saw Leeds lose at Charlton to Richard Naylor's own-goal three minutes from the end, but the Lions also lost at Tranmere.

Swindon's victory over Brentford saw them draw level on points with Millwall, going into the season's final day. United entertained Bristol Rovers at Elland Road in front of a 38,324 crowd and when Max Gradel was sent off in the 33rd minute, at first refusing to leave the field, home fans must have feared the worst.

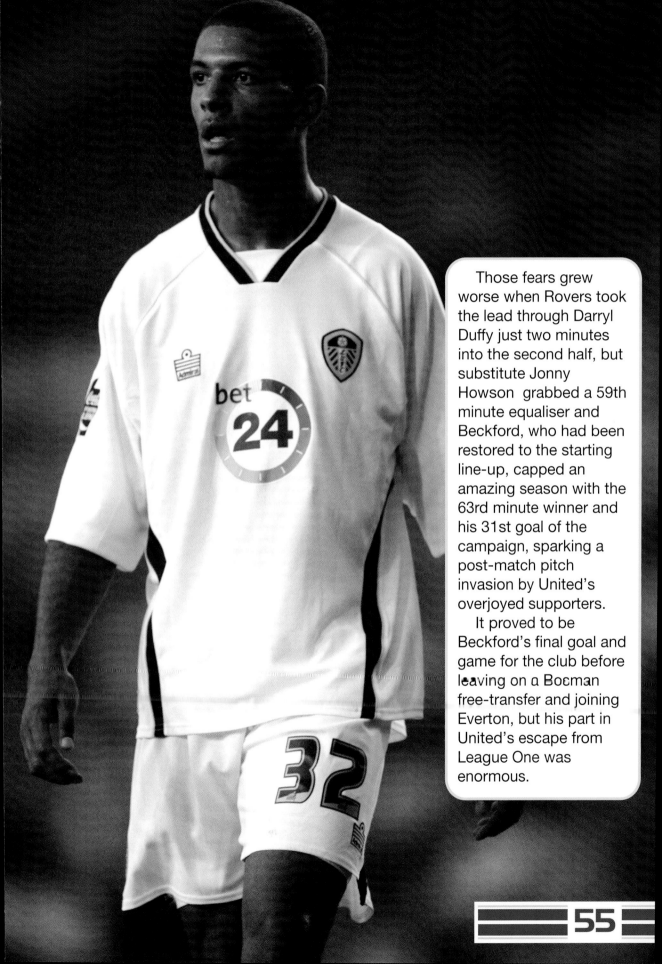

Those fears grew worse when Rovers took the lead through Darryl Duffy just two minutes into the second half, but substitute Jonny Howson grabbed a 59th minute equaliser and Beckford, who had been restored to the starting line-up, capped an amazing season with the 63rd minute winner and his 31st goal of the campaign, sparking a post-match pitch invasion by United's overjoyed supporters.

It proved to be Beckford's final goal and game for the club before leaving on a Bosman free-transfer and joining Everton, but his part in United's escape from League One was enormous.

Great Scott!
swaps red for white

When Scott Wootton decided to join Leeds United from Manchester United it was the second time in the talented defender's short career that he had made a switch between clubs whose supporters are traditional enemies.

Birkenhead-born Scott was just 16 when he turned down a youth contract at Liverpool to join their arch enemies Manchester United, the club so many Leeds fans love to hate.

Yet the former England Under 17 international reasoned that both moves were good for his career. After joining Tranmere's Centre of Excellence, Scott joined Liverpool when he was 13 and played for the Merseysiders' Under 18 team when he was just 14.

However, he felt the route towards the first team at Anfield was littered with obstacles at the time. Looking back, he said: "Leaving Liverpool for Manchester United was probably a more difficult decision than coming from Old Trafford to Leeds because I hadn't really done anything at that stage.

"Liverpool had won the Youth Cup two years running and even players from that team were struggling to get into the reserves. My path through the ranks to the first team was blocked by quite a few foreign players so I made the brave decision to move on."

Scott did play for Manchester United's first team, making his first team debut against Newcastle in a 2-1 league Cup win at Old Trafford in September, 2012. He made his Champions League debut as a second half substitute on October 2 in another 2-1 victory, this time against CFR Cluj, and later that month he conceded an injury-time penalty to send a League Cup tie against Chelsea into extra time, the Londoners eventually winning 5-4.

As so many players have done because of the fierce competition for first team places at Old Trafford, Scott was sent out on loan, with spells at his old club Tranmere, Nottingham Forest and Peterborough, but the chance to join Leeds on a three-year contract was too good to turn down.

Scott said: "Coming from Manchester United to Leeds didn't prey on my mind at all because Leeds United are a great club whose fans are so passionate. All I can do is give 100 per cent for the fans and I am sure they won't hold the Manchester United connection against me.

Scott WOOTTON

"I had a great education at Old Trafford but I felt it was the right time to move on. Hopefully I'll be getting more regular first team football at Leeds and at my age that's exactly what I need.

"The manager, Brian McDermott, came to see me play in a reserve game and once I knew he wanted to sign me it was a no-brainer because it ticked all the boxes. Things moved quite quickly early on, then it did take a while to get the deal done. I'm not sure what complications there were between the clubs but once everything was done and signed I was made up and delighted to be a Leeds United player."

McDermott believes Wootton will progress into a top class defender with the Whites and says: "It really pleased me to sign Scott. We feel he will develop with us and get better. I spoke to (Manchester United manager) David Moyes a couple of times and I have to thank him and our board of directors for making it happen.

"I spoke to two or three people who have managed Scott and they all said what a first class character he is. He really wants to improve and see his career kick on with us."

TRUE or FALSE?

1	Leeds United legend Eddie Gray has won a place in the National Football Museum's Hall of Fame.	T F
2	Roberto Mancini was sacked by Manchester City even though his side finished second in the Premier League, reached the Champions League Semi-Finals and lost the FA Cup Final.	T F
3	Brian McDermott became Leeds United's manager after coaching Leeds Rhinos.	T F
4	Wigan won the FA Cup Final but were relegated from the Premier League.	T F
5	Robert Snodgrass joined Ipswich Town when he left Leeds United.	T F
6	Sir Alex Ferguson ended his Manchester United reign with a 5-5 draw at West Ham.	T F
7	Leeds United finished the 2012-13 season 13th in the Championship.	T F
8	Steve Morison joined Leeds United from Norwich City in exchange for Luciano Becchio and cash.	T F
9	Footballer of the Year Gareth Bale was born in Swansea.	T F
10	Glasgow-born Ross McCormack played at senior level for two Scotland clubs – Rangers and Motherwell.	T F

11. Goalkeeper Peter Schmeichel played for Manchester United and Leeds United. T F

12. Michael Brown joined Leeds United from Sheffield United. T F

13. Michael Tonge arrived at Elland Road on loan from Stoke City before completing a permanent transfer. T F

14. The 2013 Champions League Final between Borussia Dortmund and Bayern Munich was the first to be contested by two German clubs. T F

15. Leeds United goalkeeper Paddy Kenny is a Scotland international. T F

16. Bayern Munich defeated Leeds United in the 1975 European Cup Final and won the 2013 Champions League. T F

17. Bradford City gained promotion from League Two to League One by defeating Burton Albion in the play-off Final at Wembley. T F

18. Leeds United were knocked out of the 2013 FA Cup by Tottenham Hotspur. T F

19. El-Hadji Diouf scored his first Leeds goal in a 3-3 home draw against Blackburn Rovers. T F

20. Sam Byram was injured in the warm-up, causing him to miss Leeds United's final home game of the 2012-13 season. T F

(Answers on Page 63).

Crewe put Luke on right track

Luke Murphy believes he couldn't have had a better place to learn his football than Crewe Alexandra's famed Centre of Excellence.

The central midfielder, who joined Leeds United in the summer for a seven-figure fee, is one of the countless players who started their careers in the railway town of Crewe before going on to better things. Seth Johnson, Luke Varney and John Pemberton are among the former Crewe players who went on to play for Leeds. And Murphy says he owes a huge debt to the coaches who set him on the right track.

He was just seven years old when he was spotted on the last day of a residential course near Crewe's ground. After a game against Crewe's Centre of Excellence team, he was invited by manager Steve Holland to train with the club for a few weeks which turned into 16 years. Luke went on to captain the Railwaymen before Leeds United manager Brian McDermott beat Wolves and Blackburn Rovers to his signature.

"Crewe has been an unbelievable place for producing players over the years," says Luke. "It's no fluke because they just keep on doing it, year in, year out. I used to watch Seth Johnson a lot when I was younger. He was Crewe's best player at the time and went for a lot of money. He had fantastic talent and would have done better at Leeds if it hadn't been for injuries.

"It would be hard to list the number of people at Crewe who helped me over the years but when I was coming through the academy Steve Holland helped me massively. He was and probably still is the biggest influence on my career. I still keep in touch with him and he helps me with any problem I have or any decision I need to make. I just need to pick up a phone and he's ready with good advice.

"Dario Gradi has been at Crewe for years and he too helped me massively. He is a great coach and, along with Neil Barker, has an immense knowledge of football. Steve Davies gave me a real confidence boost and there are two young coaches, James Collins and Neil Critchley, who are doing a great job with the academy, carrying on the tradition."

Alsager-born Luke got into football by playing with his friends in the street. He recalled: "I lived in a little village where everyone knew everyone else and at night playing football was the only thing to do. I started off as a centre forward but realised I wasn't cut out for it because I didn't have the pace. So I dropped back into central midfield and I've never regretted it.

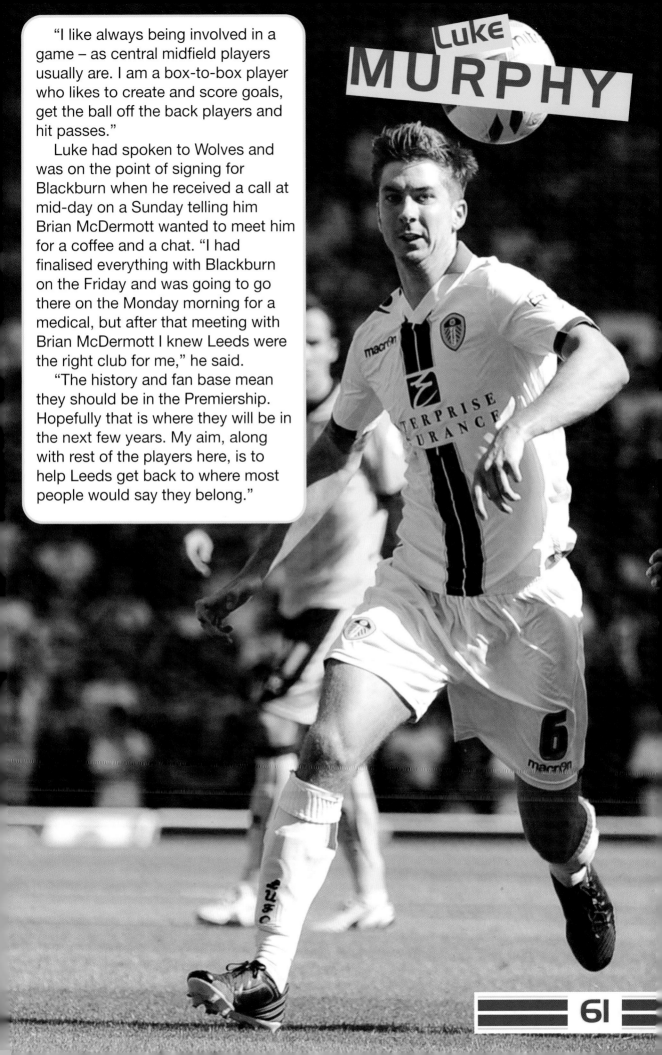

"I like always being involved in a game – as central midfield players usually are. I am a box-to-box player who likes to create and score goals, get the ball off the back players and hit passes."

Luke had spoken to Wolves and was on the point of signing for Blackburn when he received a call at mid-day on a Sunday telling him Brian McDermott wanted to meet him for a coffee and a chat. "I had finalised everything with Blackburn on the Friday and was going to go there on the Monday morning for a medical, but after that meeting with Brian McDermott I knew Leeds were the right club for me," he said.

"The history and fan base mean they should be in the Premiership. Hopefully that is where they will be in the next few years. My aim, along with rest of the players here, is to help Leeds get back to where most people would say they belong."

Luke MURPHY

Colour-in a Leeds hero

Goal ace Ross McCormack delighted United fans when he signed a new improved four-year contract before the transfer deadline, following interest from Middlesbrough and other clubs.

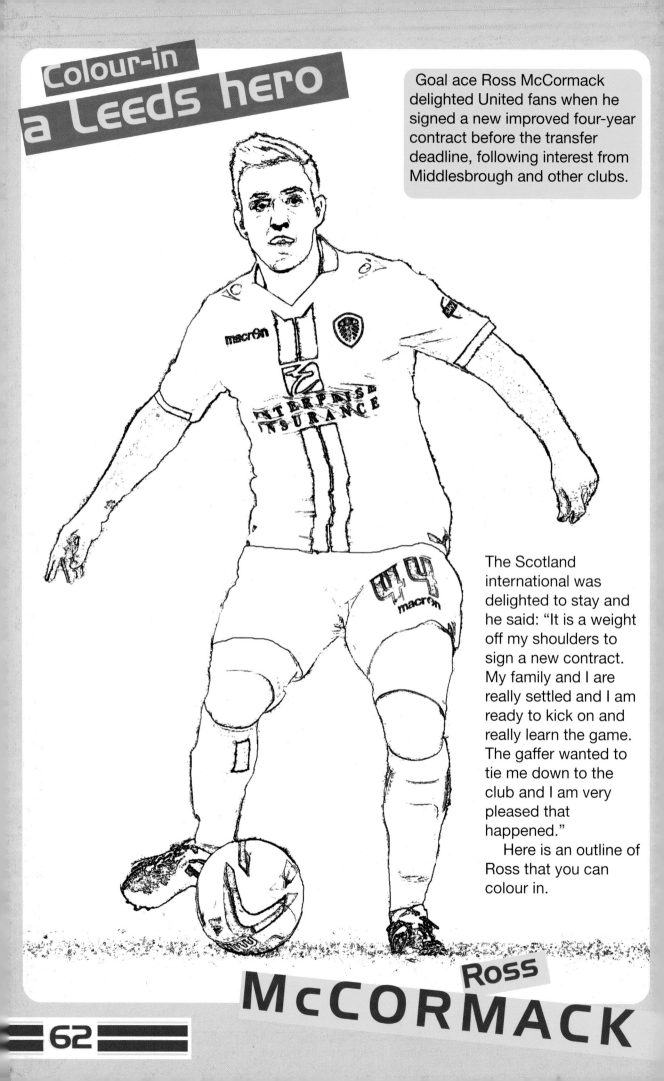

The Scotland international was delighted to stay and he said: "It is a weight off my shoulders to sign a new contract. My family and I are really settled and I am ready to kick on and really learn the game. The gaffer wanted to tie me down to the club and I am very pleased that happened."

Here is an outline of Ross that you can colour in.

Ross McCORMACK